# ABANDONED FRIEND

Sanika Hegde

First Published in December 2019

**ISBN: 978-93-5347-976-3**

**BLUEROSE PUBLISHERS**
www.bluerosepublishers.com
info@bluerosepublishers.com
+91 8882 898 898

**Cover Design:**
Pallavi Porwal

**Typographic Design:**
Namrata Saini

**Distributed by:** BlueRose, Amazon, Flipkart, Shopclues

# *From Poet's Heart:*

I would love to dedicate this book to my beloved parents for all the encouragement given to me and standing by me in all the circumstances. Their eternal faith in me is my inspiration to write. My dear mother always protected me from falling and father taught me how to get up, in case if I fall. My heartfelt thanks to both of them and their love is truly unconditional and infinite. I am indeed very fortunate to have some wonderful people around me, like a loving Principal of my school, encouraging teachers, friends and relatives who have always been supportive to me. My sincere thanks to my lovely KLE School, Manjunath Nagar, Hubballi, which moulded me and my values of life too.

# Contents

# 1. ABANDONED FRIEND

I sometimes think with all my might,
Who is the friend I have, who never dares to fight?

Poor little death, no one wants him.
They don't want him, and abandon him.
People don't know that he isn't scary,
He is gentle and humble, poor thing he is not fiery.

He has a wonderful confidence,
He goes to every house in search of a good sense.
He is always lonely; it is always 'only him!'
He doesn't have anyone; 'oh, poor him!'

When he doesn't get enough care,
He takes anyone, and we think he is a nightmare.
He is truly sweet as a pear,
For he knows what is fair and unfair.

He likes someone to be there beside him,
For everyone just abandons him.

*******

## 2. MY GOOD - OLD FRIEND

When I was about to enter Earth,
I saw someone sitting near the hearth.
I wondered who it was,
Who was blowing fire with some pause.

I asked my god, who was that,
With the black cape, bony body and a twisted hat.
God said, "You will know him soon,
For he is neither a curse nor a boon."

I went near him and stood quiet.
He seemed gentle and never did he fight.
I asked his name,
And he told his name was his fame.

He said, "I am death, who are you?"
I said, "I belong to God, I am one in few."
We spoke for some jolly time,
And it was worth diamonds and dime.

It was time for me to go to earth,
And I bid goodbye to my friend of hearth.
I was born as a baby, plumpy but small,
My tiny head was similar to a ball.

I grew up to be gentle and sensible,
I worked hard and became able.
I heard about death from people of earth,
Who was actually my friend of hearth.

People were scared of him and did not want him,
Poor death, they had abandoned him.
They never knew that he was so kind,
Even for your scolding, he would never mind.

One day suddenly, I fell ill,
Nothing worked; either medicine or pill.
I had not left my hope,
Soon I saw something black extending me a rope.

I quickly remembered my friend of hearth,
Whom I met before coming to earth.
He smiled at me and I did so too,
He sweetly asked me "How are you?"

I said I was no good,
With pills, rest and food.
He said my time had come,
And he told, "Come friend, come."

He took me out on his vehicle which was black,
I was totally blank, and his words weren't fake.
He reminded me of our talks,
Which we had around hearth and while walks.

I hugged my old friend, and off we left,
Seeing goodness, bravery, cruelty, love and theft.
I sat beside him with wonder, in his vehicle dark,
Which flew in air like in water a shark.

He reached me to the place which I had left,
Before going to the earth and here, no pain felt.
Here only God's divinity shone,
Much brighter than gold in sunshine.

I sat on silver lined cloud,
Listening to the God's heavenly words but not were they loud.
I saw my God and sat peacefully,
For I was sitting with my soul mate joyfully.

I know I am relieved from all pain,
But I was told I needed to go to be back again.
Patiently I waited for another chance to go to Earth,
Taking a promise to see me again from 'my friend of hearth.'

*******

## 3. THE BOSS OF EVERYTHING

I think I was in heaven,
And loafing about now and then.
I saw a creature holding a bag,
Some clocks, sundial, hourglass with a tag.

It seemed quite reserved,
For it did not touch anything which was served.
It was in its own world,
Without speaking even a single word.

Well, I approached it and stared its cute big eyes.
It had bells in the pocket which made jingling noise.
Its hat had flowers and flowers,
And socks were drawn lower and lower.

Its gloves were white,
And the coat was tight.
I said "Hello!", and it smiled.
Then we both went away in our own destined way.

I came to earth and grew up,
I remembered that unknown friend whom I met up.
I grew up to be a doctor and started my job,
I don't know now what that thing was up to.

One day I returned home and saw that unknown,
It was rocking on the chair and watching news.
I greeted it and said, "Hey! Hello there!"
It received my greetings with enormous happy smile.

I asked it, "What is your name?"
It said "I am time, and my name is a game."
Before I told my name it recognised me,
And told me my name!

It asked me, "You are a doctor right?"
I said, "Yes, I am one, but how do you know?"
Time said, "Well, I know everything and everyone.
I own everything and I give everything."

It said proudly, "I am not a mirror who does as you do.
I do things as per my wish.
I can do good with bad, or
Bad with good."

I asked time to stay for tea,
But time said, "I don't stop for anyone dear,
I don't wait for everyone.
I don't belong to anyone, and so I must go."

With lots of my plead, time agreed to stay.
Next day, I walked to my workplace proudly,
I now had time with me.....at my home,
When no one else had time!

I went home and discovered that time had gone.
I searched for it everywhere, but did not find it anywhere.
Then suddenly it appeared and said to me,
"My dear, finding me or trying to keep me is foolishness."

It said, "I don't limit my challenges,
I challenge my limits.
I begin from the end and open at close.
I can change everything, anyone, anyplace."

I saw, death roaming about without a victim,
And I asked him "Hey, do you know this time?"
Suddenly death fell at his knees, saluted time and said,"
"Greetings my master, order me."

Time said, "Death is my junior; everyone is scared of him,
And he is scared of me.
He brings to me, whom I ask him to bring,
My orders do not end; they are endless like a ring."

Lastly time said proudly in a serious tone,
"I created the universe and I shall destroy it.
You cannot predict me or my job.
What you can do is only sit and watch me."

Saying this, time vanished with a jingling noise.
Death came closer to me and said,
"Hey friend, my master is the boss of everything."
Death had gone too, and I was standing dumbstruck,
Wondering whether 'my' time had come or not!

*******

# 4. UNDER THE GROUND

Who is under the ground I think,
Staring at the moon, without a blink.
We burry the human body under the ground,
And keep garlands round and round.

The soul goes up when the body is down.
And the body gets up when the soul is down.
In life, we see many ups and downs,
Just like the body and soul.

Don't feel low because your value is high.
Don't care about the comments of a passer-by.
After you die, your body loves ground and soul loves sky.
Do some great things when alive, as high as sky.

Soul and body have different ways.
One reaches sky and one falls on ground.
Follow your dreams and them if you chase.
You will be as high as sky even on ground.

*******

# 5. I AND ME

I saw someone, one day,
On first week of May.
I saw her again in the swimming pool,
Wondering whether I was a fool.

I stared at her quietly,
She stared at me calmly.
I saw her again so much more,
She saw me too without any bore.

I liked her good nature,
And hoped to see her in future.
I think I even saw her in past,
My memories vanishing fast.

One day I discovered,
What she too had discovered.
We both looked same,
We had the same name.

I waved at her, and she too did with a coat of fur.
I saw her in pool, mirror and glass, but never in class.
That is when I came to know that she was me,
I was her and so it be.

*******

# 6. HOW TO BELIEVE OTHERS?

I was in a very hot and sunny desert,
With no breakfast, lunch or dinner.
There were sand dunes, sand and sand,
Also cactus, dates and palm trees.

I was exhausted and so did my camel,
For there was not a single drop of water to drink.
The sun was blazing hot on head,
Under me there was only sand, not mud.

My camel ran away and I was loafing,
I was left alone searching and moaning.
My eyes saw a huge lake of water,
My throat exclaimed "Oasis!"

I ran with my might,
I thought I would drink a lot of water and settle there at night.
I ran with my mind filled with watery thoughts,
For I would be living near the water- 'my life'.

But, it was a mirage,
My body was filled with fury and rage.
I regretted for trusting my eyes,
For I hoped for something as cool as ice.

I got cheated by myself,
My eyes broke my faith.
I thought "When I got cheated by own eyes,
How can I believe some unknown?"
'When I cheated me,
How can some other not?

*******

# 7. HOW I FELL IN LOVE.......

He kept staring at me and my eyes,
With his crystal brown eyes.
His eyes were glowing like a star,
Saying 'everything's fair in love and war'.

His jet black hair swayed in the air,
And his face was bright and fair.
His teeth were beautiful and white,
Which sparkled like diamond at night.

He was tall and muscular,
He seemed to be kind and familiar.
I was mesmerised by his smiles,
It would take me miles and miles.

Well, that day I went home,
With his memories fluffy like a foam.
His home was in front of mine,
It was huge, beautiful and fine.

He stood in the balcony with his gleaming sight,
He seemed so gentle, he never was to fight.
He saw me and so did I,
We stared at each other, eye to eye.

Many days went by, and we met one day,
We saw each other, smiled and just passed by.
We stared each other in silence, those moments were magical
for it meant so much.
I felt feeble winds blowing, and butterflies in my stomach.

He came with me everywhere,
He would be in joy when he was with me.
One day, some strangers followed me,
My silent love came and stood for me.

He was so brave and strong,
He fought with those whose intention was wrong.
He risked his life for me,
For his love who was me.

From that day on, I believed him a lot,
For he wasn't cunning to plan a plot.
We went together for strolls,
And played games with discs and balls.

He loved to play and so did I,
We never liked to wish each other goodbye.
We spent together every evening,
And woke up with each other's thoughts in the morning.

He has a special place in my heart,
And I know that we will never part.
He is my love and I am his,
When he's with me, I feel eternal bliss.

We meet, laugh and enjoy every day,
He cheers me up every day.
This is how I fell in love,
With my fantastic true love.

My love loves to play on ground and bog,
For he is a cute and lovely dog.

*******

# 8. WHERE IS MY LIFE?

I was wondering about me,
And then, I saw my life flying and fidgeting with something.
It was holding two balls- happiness and sadness.
Its bag was filled with pain and relief.

It came to me and asked `What do you want-
Happiness or sadness, pain or relief?
Tell me dear, and I shall give it to you.
Speak the truth, and receive your wishes'

I was surprised because life did only what it wanted,
It never listened to me before.
I at once doubted,
Whether it was a trick of life on me.

I replied, `Give me anything you like'
Life was pleased.
It said, `Because you are brainy, I'll tell you a secret,
My dear, never ever trust me.'

It continued 'Yes. You heard that right.
Don't believe in me.
Those who believed in me are nowhere now.
I am a teacher and I am a cheater.'
It started again, `I make things difficult for you.
I make you fall down and cry.
I lift you up when you are hurt.
I am always with you, but you are in my game'.

I asked, `Why are you so painful sometimes?'
Life said, `That's because, you try to look after me.
Just look after you, which is possible, and I promise
I will look after you'.

I asked 'When will you end? Does death come to you too?'
Life laughed and replied, `When I do not live, how can I
die dear?
I fight with death for you.
But, since time is my friend, after a long struggle, I let death
take you away.'

Life quoted with pride 'When time created the universe,
It sent me on to earth the first.
I was the beginning of everything.
After some period, so that I should not stay with only one
thing for long,
Death came and waged a war against me.
Sometimes I won and many a times I lost.'

Saying this, life gave me one beautiful ball,
Which was continuously rotating.
It said its last sentence 'Take this, this is an epic ball-
Ball of understanding universe.
Meet you soon, until then be yourself.'
Saying this, life opened his huge wings and rushed into me.
I suddenly felt a sense of rebirth.

*******

# 9. THE BEAUTY OF VISION

'The pearls are showered from the sky,
The clouds seem like pure floating cotton.
The silver is gushing downwards,
The gold and red rubies are swaying in the air.
Hey, peasant come look at this mesmerising scene.' said the poet.

The peasant came out of the window and saw.
He burst out laughing and asked the poet;
'Hey young man, are you out of your mind?
You said pearls, silver, gold, rubies and whatever...
Where have they all gone? I can see only –
My tulips, roses, the river and its raining!'

At that time the poet turned towards the peasant and he saw his pet
He exclaimed 'Such a cute tiny fluffy ball,
Hello little one, you look like a cotton ball.
Your tiny sparkling stars amaze me,
Your honest little smile soothes me'

The peasant yelled, 'Don't you recognise a cat?
Your rumbling rubbish, you man.
Look, if you have some problem, please see a doctor.
But please do not trouble me.'

The poet said 'It's all about the beauty of vision peasant,
Some see a coin, but some see a treasure.
I am one of those who sees a treasure.

It is not about how your eyes look, it is about how your eyes
see the world.'
Saying so, poet started singing, and the peasant still
confused,
Stared at his own eyes in the mirror.

*******

## 10. ONE MEANS EVERYONE

I remember my heart telling me,
'I who wrote this poem,
You who is reading this poem,
They on whom is this poem,
We who understand the motto of this poem- are all one.'

With red blood running,
With one heart beating,
With one mind thinking,
With one god we have,
All are one.

All are one, one for all, all for one,
We are all one, not the only one.
Different we are only in our dharma,
One we are all in our karma.
When karma is greater than dharma,
One is greater than different.

No matter how we are or where we live,
Who we are or whom we have,
Why we are or where we are,
What we are or how we are,
What we have gained or what we have lost,
At the end, still, we all are one.

Apart from hatred or jealousy,
Cast or creed, religion or gender,
Betrayal or threat, there still exists –
Love and care, faith and trust,
Truth and belief, because we all are one.

*******

# 11. THE TREE LIFE

The tree was huge and strong,
With dark branches and swaying leaves.
The fruits were loosened and hanging from the tree,
The flowers were budding and the buds were glowing.
The roots held the tree strong, and the tree was strong and finc.

Many birds and the squirrels lived on the tree,
They munched the fruits and were grateful to the tree.
These tiny tots loved the tree and were grateful to the tree.
The giant and the tiny tots were best friends for they helped each other always.

Many men rested under the tree, ate fruits, plucked flowers,
And sang merrily and went home.
The next day they brought a very sharp axe,
And started jabbing the tree.

The fruits fell, the flowers got earthed,
The branches broke, and the leaves flew away.
But, the tiny tots would not leave the tree,
For they loved each other dearly.

The men of course could not even touch the roots,
For the roots were strong and confident.
The tiny tots did not leave the tree until its last breath,
But at last, when it was gone, they ran away weeping.

Our life also is like a tree.
The stem of the tree is our life which gets cut one day.

The roots of the tree is our soul which is unbreakable and uncontrollable.
The tiny tots are our family and friends. They are the dear ones,
Who always are there for us.

The men are cheaters, jabbers, betrayers who cheat us and can cause death.
The fruits are success which comes only at certain times and it falls down easily.
The buds are our hidden talents which will bloom one day.
The branches are the responsibilities which keep on growing.
The leaves are the opportunities which fly away far.

All the fruits, flowers, leaves, branches, buds, men, stem-
Will get destroyed.
Only the roots and tiny tots remain,
That is 'the soul' and loved ones will be immortal.

*******

# 12. THE UNIVERSE

The place which no one knew,
The time when no one lived, which no one dreamt,
The place where nothing was,
Are we calling it, the 'UNIVERSE'?

Universe was something formed out of nothing.
Filled with millions of celestial bodies today,
Was not the same when it was that day.
Beyond the imagination is the place,
Which is called the universe.

A black thing from somewhere jumped nowhere,
It was sky who felt too bad to be too plain,
It was the sky who decorated itself,
With millions of shiny things.

These shiny things were now alive.
They were the stars who shine always,
They were the stars who formed huge groups,
The groups are today called galaxies, and ours was the
'milky way'.

Some stars formed groups only of few,
These are known as constellations.
These were the constellations who formed a pattern.
These were the constellations who are shining at night.

The stars felt sick and puked,
And out came the dust and gases,

These were the dust and gases which floated in the space,
These were the dust and gases who formed round balls.

Many round balls scattered here and there,
Some of them fell in the milky way.
These were the planets who were born out of stars,
These were the planets on whom we live.

These planets were emotional.
Mercury and Venus were the angriest,
Earth and mars were moderate and calm,
Saturn and Jupiter were very naughty,
Uranus and Neptune were too reserved.

These were the planets, who always wanted to be their way,
These were the planets, who never obeyed the stars.
These were the planets, who annoyed everyone.
These were the planets, who were too naughty.

The stars chanted a spell with anger to bring someone,
This someone would be the one to control the planets.
This someone would be the one who would be strong and
fierce.
This someone was born out of anger.

This someone was the 'SUN'
Sun was the one who was burning and angry.
Sun was the one who controlled the planets,
Sun was the one who made the stars happy.

Slowly, planets started crying because of sun.
Planets were the ones who asked the stars to bring a friend.

Stars calmly chanted a spell to bring someone
who would be a friend.
This someone would be a company for sun.

This someone was the 'MOON',
Moon was the one who created joy.
Moon was the one who was sun's friend,
Moon was the one who made the house a home.

The sun placed Mercury and Venus in front of him,
Earth and Mars next to them, Saturn and
Jupiter behind them,
And Uranus and Neptune at the back.
Little Pluto was a new born baby and he had freedom to
move anywhere.

Sun gradually became the ultimate power.
He created life on earth and on earth only.
He gave the powers to stars to twinkle,
And gave some of his powers to moon.

After some million years, the living things on earth,
Started destroying her.
Sun asked her to cause disasters,
But she was so kind that she did only little.

Then sun said, 'Before the selfish creatures,
Would go to any of you, we shall get blasted.
Then, we will get formed again,
And never form such selfish ones'.

Moon added 'Then, every one of us would be happy,
And now let's be how we are,

And wait for that time.'
Everyone cheered up.

So, after some million years from now,
Things will go, and come back again in universe.
But, if we keep on hurting earth in every step,
It will not be long that earth will burst before her time.

*******

# 13. EVERY DAY IS A BIRTHDAY!

Do not be afraid of growing old,
For you still have the heart of the child.
Do not be afraid of nearing death,
For you have a life which you have truly lived.

Do not be worried of your old grey hair,
For your thoughts are still younger.
Do not be tensed of your failures,
For your success is more than that.'

Do not be sad of your past,
For your future is bright.
Do not be scared of the difficulties,
For your soul is pure and divine.

Celebrate today for it is your day.
Remember your days of joy and happiness.
Rejoice the fact that you were born for a purpose.
Today was a day, when a great soul was born.

Your loved ones,
Family and friends feel proud,
For they have a wonderful spirit with them.
Feel proud, for you are the ideal one for them.

Be grateful to god for god has given you many dear ones,
Learn from the days of pain,

And unleash the thoughts of sorrow,
For you have greater things to do.

Remember, you will rejoice every day,
If you feel that every day is your 'Happy Birth Day'!

*******

# 14. ANIMALITY

When I am with animals, I am filled with joy,
For they truly spread joy around.
When I am with animals, I feel proud,
For they make me feel I am a good soul.

When I am with animals, I am truly me,
For they do not judge me.
When I am with animals, I forget all my pain,
For they wash away all my sorrows.

When I am with animals, I experience love,
For they love me with their heart.
When I am with animals, I feel positive,
For they never are cunning.

When I am with animals, I can share all my words,
For they never question me.
When I am with animals, I feel free and pure,
For they never lecture me.

Well, many of us feel like this with animals,
Because they do not have humanity.
All of us feel great with animals,
For they have in them 'animality'.

Once upon a time, long long ago,
Love, care, share, positivity, empathy, well-wishing, helping
Were labelled as 'Humanity', and
Killing, hunting, fighting, madness, wildness was labelled as
'Animality'.

But today, long long years after,
The titles have reversed.
The animals are now the selfless creatures,
And the humans are the selfish creatures.

Humans have created nothing except pollution,
They have caused disasters, and are filled with pride.
The selfless creatures come to know about our deeds,
And still we don't even think of realising it.

Animals are the first ones to help, in any accident,
Whereas humans are busy clicking photos and making videos.
Humans start hating a species of animals, only if they use self-defence,
And animals even when humans torture them, never hate anyone.

On this earth, if everything has to get all right,
'Humanity' must end,
And a new reign of 'Animality' must begin,
Where its true value is worshipped.

Unlike humans, animals do not have conflicts with their 'Dharma',
They are very happy, only with their 'Karma'.

*******

# 15. THE EPIC PERIOD

When I was born, life was with me.
Time created me and sent life with me.
Time told life that I would face two powerful things soon-
Love and death.

Life gave me joy and pride,
Life gave me pain and sorrow.
Life taught me the value of winning,
And the experience of losing.

I grew up, and I met love.
When I met love, I forgot my life.
Love left me in a world of fantasy,
A world where I lived in dream.

Love was like an infection,
Spreading from one person to another.
Like infection, itching felt good,
But left behind a big mark.

For sometime, love was good,
But then, it left me.
I came back in the real world,
But I felt bitter, for now love was gone.

I thought of quitting,
But I did not have enough courage.
I tried to quit,
And I was drowned in sorrow.

Death felt happy, for now it got a victim.
It came near me and tried to take me away.
That time, life came and kicked death.
Death fell far away and stared at life.

Life was young and strong.
Death was neither young nor old.
Death waged a war against life.
Life fought bravely for me and defeated death.

Death said 'Life, I will not forget this defeat,
I will come again, in your old time.
I need this little girl.
I will take her away when she becomes an old granny.
Be ready.'

Many years, I lived a happy life,
A happy life with my loved ones.
A good and satisfactory life,
A life which I felt contented when I remembered.

Many years later, I grew up to be an old granny.
A granny with old grey hair,
A granny with wrinkled skin,
A granny with some memories lost.
Death came again.
Now, it looked strong and confident.
It was now experienced,
As it had taken away many people, and defeated life many times.

Life appeared again.
Life looked old now.
It fell many times when it started a fight with death,

Life was about to lose, when suddenly time appeared.
Since time was life's friend, life had to listen to time.

Time asked life to come with it.
Life slowly left my hand with tears.
It said 'see you again dear. Goodbye.'
And I went away silently with death.

At last, death was successful.
Life became young again, when it went with someone else.
Time started planning for a new person.
No one won and no one lost.

*******

## *The End*

www.ingramcontent.com/pod-product-compliance
Ingram Content Group UK Ltd.
Pitfield, Milton Keynes, MK11 3LW, UK
UKHW042001190726
13854UKWH00005B/2114

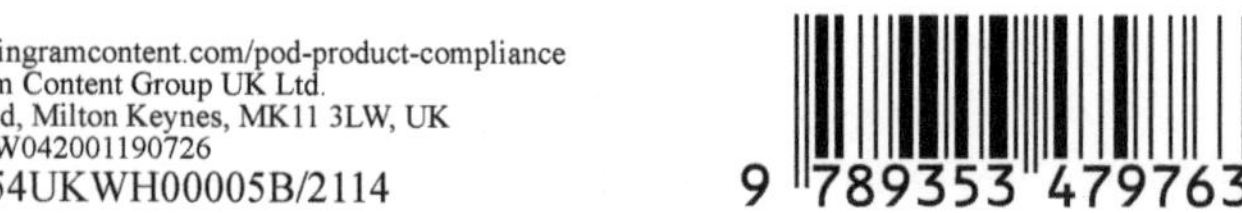

9 789353 479763